Magnetta Diamond
and the Skate Mates

Written by
Heather Pindar

Illustrated by
Ronaldo Barata

'Magnetta Diamond and the Skate Mates'
An original concept by Heather Pindar
© Heather Pindar 2024

Illustrated by Ronaldo Barata

Published by MAVERICK ARTS PUBLISHING LTD
Suite 1, Hillreed House, 54 Queen Street,
Horsham, West Sussex, RH13 5AD
© Maverick Arts Publishing Limited September 2024
+44 (0)1403 256941

A CIP catalogue record for this book is available at the British Library.

ISBN 978-1-83511-037-9

Printed in India

www.maverickbooks.co.uk

Chapter 1
From Daydreamer to Superhero

In their secret headquarters, the Anti-Evil Squad crowded around their computers.

"That supervillain Outa Sight is out of control," said the team leader, Ayo Bundi. "She must be stopped!"

"Yes, look! Her mini bots are causing chaos all over the world," said equipment designer, Ben Shaw.

James Scanlon, the research assistant, rubbed his chin. "Hacked computers, jammed roads, power cuts... But how do you stop an invisible supervillain?"

Ben nodded towards Margaret Stone, their brilliant lead scientist. She was staring into a glass tube full of a bright green mixture. "What do you think, Margaret?"

"Okay, Margaret," said James, his feet crunching over the rocky rim of the volcano. "The Explorer Pod is ready to take you down to the core now. Have you got everything you need?"

"Er, I think so," said Margaret, patting her pockets. "I've got my special mixture for harvesting the magnetic powers. Anyone got a tissue? Volcanoes always make my nose run."

"You can't blow your nose with your helmet on," said Ayo. Margaret climbed into the sturdy metal pod that would carry her into the core of the volcano.

Ben leaned inside the pod to speak to Margaret. "If it gets too hot or you hear rumbling, get straight back in the pod and come up."

"Okay, will do," said Margaret.

"Good luck!" called Ayo.

"Thanks! **Achoo! ACHOO!**" sneezed Margaret as she closed the door to the pod.

★★★

After a while, the scientists began to worry.

"How long has Margaret been down there?" asked Ayo.

James looked at his computer screen. "One hour and fifty-two minutes. It's a bit longer than I expected."

"She has to pump her special mixture into all the cracks in the rock," said Ben. "Margaret said it might take a long time for the mixture to harness the volcano's magnetic powers."

Suddenly, Ben looked up. "I'm picking up noises on the seismograph!" He was looking at the paper running out of the seismograph, a machine that shows tremors in the earth. "Maybe Margaret's new mixture is working."

"Yes, hopefully it's scooping up all that super-magnetic power right now," said Ayo.

A moment later there was a loud rumble followed by a big explosion. Orange sparks and a cloud of dark smoke floated out of the volcano.

Ayo yelled into the smoke, "Margaret! Are you alright?"

9

Chapter 2
Mini Bot Emergency

A week later, Magnetta had practised using her new magnetic superpowers and was ready for action.

"There you go, Magnetta," said Ben. "I've made you a padded case for the diamond. You can clip it to your belt. And here's a spare for when the other one's in the wash."

"Thanks, Ben, you think of everything!" said Magnetta, laughing. "It would be a disaster if I lost the diamond."

"Right, we're getting reports of Outa Sight's bots attacking the airport again," said James. "No planes can fly in or out."

"My first mission! I'm on my way!" said Magnetta.

"How will you get to the airport?" said Ben.

"Watch me! If I reverse my magnetic power, I can hover like this."

"Very nice. I don't understand it, but cool," said Ben.

"I'll explain it to you later," laughed Magnetta. "It's hard work, though. Hovering wears me out."

"Good luck, Magnetta!" said Ben. He handed her the two diamond cases again. "Don't forget these. You left them on your desk!"

Magnetta zoomed to the airport. As soon as she walked into the building, her magnetic powers began attracting Outa Sight's mini bots.

PING! PING! PING! The bots stuck to her clothes.

Magnetta peeled the bots off, then stomped on them. Afterwards, Magnetta rubbed the diamond to switch off her magnetic powers.

Soon the airport was running normally again. People clapped and cheered when they saw Magnetta. She waved as she hurried past. As Magnetta left the building, she heard a rustle behind her. She looked around but all she could see was a faint red mist. *Strange*, thought Magnetta.

She saw the number 39 bus pull up in front of the airport and quickly jumped on. *I need a rest from hovering*, she thought.

Magnetta chose a seat upstairs. She put the diamond into its case. She was about to zip it up and clip it onto her belt when the bus crossed the river. *Hmm*, she thought, *I wonder if I can hover over water?*

Magnetta sighed happily and began daydreaming.

Chapter 3
Skate Mates are Go!

Meanwhile at the Marsh Skateboard Park, a group of skateboarders were practising their tricks. The friends called themselves the Skate Mates.

"Hey, nice ollie!" shouted Tessanne as Ravi landed perfectly from his jump.

"Thanks!" said Ravi.

"Me and Tessanne are taking a break," said Fay.

Ravi and Sam joined them on a steep grassy bank. They watched as a boy walked by with a skateboard under his arm. A small hairy dog ran beside him.

"Nice dog!" said Ravi. "What's his name?"

"Scout," said the boy.

"He's my assistance dog. He helps me chill when everything gets too much."

"That's really cool!" said Fay. "We're the Skate Mates. What's your name?"

"Dequan. Scout does tricks. Do you want to see them?"

"Oh yeah," said Sam. "We *love* tricks."

"Okay," said Dequan. He looked at Scout. "Scout! Gloves!"

Scout sniffed Dequan's hand. He began to pull gently at the fingers. In a few moments, he had pulled off both gloves. The Skate Mates cheered.

"Scout!" said Dequan again. "Pocket!"

Scout sniffed Dequan's jacket pocket. He pulled out his phone. "Good dog!" said Dequan.

"Your dog is so cool!" said Sam. "How did you..."

CLANK! SCREECH! CLUNK!

Everyone looked towards the noise.

A strange beast covered in bits of metal was staggering across the park. It stumbled over its own feet and fell over.

16

"What did you say, Dequan?" said Fay.

"Scout can find Outa Sight," said Dequan. "He just needs something that smells of Magnetta. Then he can track down the smell of her on the diamond."

"And Outa Sight has the diamond so he'll find Outa Sight too," said Fay. "Right, Dequan?"

"Right!" said Dequan.

Magnetta wiggled her hand between the pieces of metal stuck to her. "Take this," she said. "It's my spare diamond case. The other one looks just like it. It's got my scent on it. Put my number in your phones and keep me posted! Look out for red mist too. Outa Sight gets a red mist around her... I think it's when she's angry."

Dequan held the spare diamond case towards Scout's nose. "Find it, Scout!" he said. "Find it!"

The Skate Mates ran to collect their boards. Dequan hesitated.

"Come on, Dequan," said Fay. "You'll be much quicker on your board."

"I'm not very good," said Dequan, "I won't keep up

with you."

"Just try," said Fay. "Look! Scout's waiting for you."

Dequan saw that Scout was sitting on the grass looking at him. **"GO Scout!"** said Dequan, pushing off on his board. **"Find it!"**

Scout began to run. The Skate Mates sped along the concrete path after Scout. Fay looked back and saw Dequan beginning to drop behind them.

"Quicker but lighter pushes, Dequan," she called.

Dequan took a breath. He pushed more gently with his right leg. Suddenly he found it was easier to push faster, and his board began to pick up speed.

"Thanks, Fay!" he shouted. They followed Scout up the tarmac path to the housing estate.

The Skate Mates and Dequan stopped. They were in a walkway between two tower blocks. Scout was running in a tight circle and barking.

"I think Scout's found Outa Sight!" whispered Dequan. "Can you try and make Outa Sight angry?"

"Yeah," said Tessanne quietly, "we can do some trick moves around Outa Sight. She doesn't need to know we're trying to get the diamond, right?"

The others gave her the thumbs up. Sam did an ollie near to where he guessed Outa was standing. Fay tried a noisy powerslide on the opposite side. Then the Mates practised their jumps and turns all over the walkway.

Slowly, a red mist rose and formed a faint, fuzzy body shape. One by one, the mates noticed it and then quickly looked away, grinning.

Fay stopped her board next to Dequan. "It's just like Magnetta said!" she whispered. "Outa Sight goes all red and misty when she's angry. Ha! She didn't like our board tricks."

"And now we can see where she is," grinned Dequan.

Dequan saw his chance to trick Outa Sight. He took the spare diamond case from his pocket. He threw it down close to Outa Sight's red mist. The red mist hurried forward and bent low to pick it up.

Fooled you, thought Dequan.

"Scout! Pocket!" he said, pointing at the stooping mist.

Scout quickly jumped onto his hind legs and thrust his nose at the misty shape. When he landed, his mouth was empty.

"Oi! Get off me, dog!" hissed Outa Sight, turning around.

"Pocket!" said Dequan again, desperately. He pointed to the other side of the red mist. Scout moved over and jumped up again.

When Scout's feet touched the floor, Dequan could see he had a black case in his mouth. He'd got the other case from Outa Sight's pocket! Now to check it definitely had the diamond...

"There goes Outa Sight!" said Sam. "She panicked and ran into that bin cupboard!"

The Skate Mates jumped off their boards and leaned against the door.

"We've got Outa Sight, Magnetta," shouted Ravi into his phone, "and the diamond."

Everyone heard Magnetta's scream of joy.

"We'll come back to the park and switch off your magnetic powers as soon as we can," said Ravi.

"Great! Thanks," said Magnetta. "I'm phoning the Anti-Evil Squad now. They'll be down to pick up Outa Sight," she said.

A moment later, Ravi's phone buzzed again.

"Er, it's me," said Magnetta. "I forgot to ask, where are you exactly?"

Chapter 5
Outa Sight is Outa Time

The TV studio was crowded. The presenter turned to Magnetta and said, "So Magnetta, you've had enormous success on your first mission."

"Yes, Outa Sight is in prison. She won't be able to release any more of her horrible bots," said Magnetta smiling.

"Yes, we're all very glad about that," said the presenter. "It must have been a huge surprise to find out she had special clothes to make her invisible."

Magnetta nodded. "Yes, they mix with the chemicals in her skin to make her disappear."

"And it must have been an even bigger surprise to find her trapped in a bin cupboard!"

There was a gasp as Magnetta's words sank in.

"Some brave and clever people tracked Outa Sight," she said. "They tricked her. They got my diamond back. And they locked Outa Sight in the bin cupboard. They are the real heroes. And here they are now!"

The Skate Mates walked onto the stage, blinking in the bright lights. The presenter rushed over.

"Who are you? Did you really catch Outa Sight?"

"We're the Skate Mates," said Fay, "I'm Fay, this is Sam, Ravi, Tessanne and our new members, Dequan and Scout. And yes, we really caught Outa Sight."

"And they are happy to help me track down Putrid Pong and any other evil supervillains!" said Magnetta.

Suddenly, everyone in the room stood up. They began to cheer and clap. The Skate Mates joined hands and lifted their arms, laughing.

Magnetta rushed forward to join them. She tripped. The pink diamond flew through the air.

PLONK! It landed in the presenter's lap.

"Oops! Sorry!" said Magnetta.

The End

WHAT NEXT?

Did you enjoy this Fusion Reader? If you are looking for more, the Maverick Reading Scheme is a bright, attractive range of books with plenty of stories for everyone. All titles are book-banded for guided reading to the industry standard and edited by a leading educational consultant.

MAVERICK FUSION READERS

To view the whole Maverick Reading Scheme, visit our website at

www.maverickearlyreaders.com

Or scan the QR code to view our scheme instantly!